THREE LITTLE OWLS

Quentin Blake * Emanuele Luzzati

John Yeoman

THREE
LITTLE OWLS

Tate Publishing

With a bop and a bip and a bip and a bop
A wardrobe with three little owls on the top.
And each of the three has decided to lay
A shiny white egg as it's Christmas today.

One put on an apron, and one a smart dress,
(And why would they do that?
I'm sure you can't guess.)
The third thought she'd do even better than that –
She's wearing a gigantic vase for a hat.

They found a huge barrel, so each of them took
A rod and a line and a paperclip hook.

In less than five minutes they'd landed a bite —
A fish so amazing it gave them a fright.

With green wings and glasses he hasn't the look
Of something you'd normally find on a hook.

He's writing some speeches (although he can't speak)
In languages ranging from Hindi to Greek.

That's so much excitement they'd all had in May,
From June to September they fluttered away
To dance on the rooftops and hoot with delight
For much of the day and for all of the night.

In warm August sunshine (forget about rain)
Our three little owls were relaxing again.

With a bop and a bip and a bip and a bop
A wardrobe with three little owls on the top.

The holiday's ended and school must begin.
The three little owls fly away to Berlin,
And then to Australia, and then to Peru,
They flew and they flew and they flew and they flew;

They crossed every desert, they crossed every sea –
In England for breakfast, in China for tea.

With a bop and a bip
And a bip and a bop.
The rains have arrived now –
There's no sign they'll stop.

Beneath his umbrella the fish starts to fret:
Despite his new raincoat he's going to get wet.
He really detests getting caught in a storm,
So puts on his gloves and his shoes to keep warm.

With a bop and a bip and a bip and a bop,
A wardrobe with one soggy fish on the top.
He sits there alone and forlorn in his mac
And wishes the three little owls would come back.

Then just before Christmas the fish catches sight
Of three little owls flying home through the night.

And what is it brings that warm flush to his cheeks?
It's what he can see in the little owls' beaks:

A jumbo-sized basket brimful of fine treats
Like raisins and almonds and turkey and sweets
And apples and ice-cream and chocolates galore;
A real Christmas feast – who could ever want more!

My poem's now finished – I've come to a stop
With a bop

        and a bip

            and a bip

                and a bop.

Emanuele Luzzati was a celebrated illustrator, set and stage designer, and animator. His reputation was international but he lived all his life in the house in Genoa where he was born.

After his death in 2007 all his artwork and papers were transferred to the Museo Luzzati, a sixteenth-century fortified building on the port of Genoa. Amongst these works was a manuscript entitled 'Filastrocca di Natale', which he had written and no doubt one day intended to illustrate.

Quentin Blake is an illustrator whose work has appeared in hundreds of books, both for children and adults, as well as in museums and hospitals.

In 2006 he was invited to show his work alongside that of Emanuele Luzzati at the Italian Embassy in London, and later, in 2009, to present it in an exhibition at the Museo Luzzati in Genoa. At the end of the exhibition Quentin Blake was asked if he would take on the task of illustrating 'Filastrocca'. Here it is, in an English version by John Yeoman, who has provided the words for many other of Quentin Blake's books, and with the English title of *Three Little Owls*.

First published 2013 by order of the Tate Trustees
by Tate Publishing, a division of Tate Enterprises Ltd,
Millbank, London SW1P 4RG
www.tate.org.uk/publishing

Original Italian text © Nugae Srl 2013
English text © John Yeoman 2013
Artwork © Quentin Blake 2013

Reprinted 2014

A catalogue record for this book is available from the British Library

ISBN 978 1 84976 080 5

Designed by Arteprima | www.arteprima.com
Colour reproduction by DL Imaging Ltd, London
Printed in China by Toppan Leefung

Cover artwork by Quentin Blake

MIX
Paper from
responsible sources
FSC
www.fsc.org   FSC® C104723